Dedicated with love to Joyce, Sophie, and
my parents Cyril and Pearl.

Marty Baker

To my wife and partner Joanne and our
children, Kate and Zack. And my parents
Bot and Jean, who from as far back as I can
remember, always encouraged my talent.
And to all the free Peteys in the world.

Bot Roda

The Pirate Island Cast

Gabe

The son of the island's most famous parrot family and the leading cadet at the Semper Fly Pirate Academy.

Ponce

Gabe's loyal companion and fellow cadet who can't resist a clawful of crackers.

Patch

The Pirate Academy's crusty old drill sergeant famous for his eye patch and peg leg.

Captain Sikes

The legendary pirate captain who comes to Parrot Island to select a new parrot for his ship.

Dragut

A large hawk and the feared first mate of the pirate ship the Rusty Cutlass.

Bilge

The brave, ship smart rat living secretly aboard the Rusty Cutlass.

Barney

A barnacle who has lived his entire life on the ship and knows just about everything about pirates.

Little Bart

The island's pint-sized lookout who dreams of becoming a cadet

Pearl

Pearl is a half English, half French female pirate who meets with Sikes on the high seas.

Fabiola

Crafty and swashbuckling, she is the parrot of the notorious female pirate, Pearl de Montauban.

You need to be a pirate to see it. But hidden off the coast of South America is a tiny jewel of an island. It's called Parrot Island or Isla de Papagayos. For generations, pirates have sworn a blood oath not to reveal the location.

After all, this secret place is where pirates get their parrots. Not just your average squawking feather head, but a fine parrot destined to perch atop a captain's shoulder.

Gabriel stood near the top of the bell tower – the highest point on the island. It was his favorite place to watch the pirate ships come into the harbor below. Gabe, as he was known to his friends, was training to be a pirate's parrot.

But he wasn't sure he wanted to become a pirate. He didn't want to disappoint his father, the legendary Sir Cyril Edwards, the swashbuckling hero of Blackbeard's crew. He loved the island and didn't want to leave.

"G--A --B?" A raspy, out-of-breath squawk came from inside the tower. Gabe looked down and saw a claw-full of crackers reach the top of the ladder. Then, a large feathered head. It was his best friend and loyal companion, Ponce.

"Gabe, hurry, we'll be late for drills."

Every parrot's dream is to attend the Semper Fly Academy. It could turn a green recruit (or any color actually) into a parrot that could fly in a hurricane, navigate dangerous seas, and seek treasure.

But most of all, the academy taught young cadets how to band together as a crew.

"Avast ye," bellowed Patch. "You're all just a bunch of baggywrinkles!"

Patch was the feared drill parrot of the Semper Fly Academy. A veteran of many pirate voyages, he had a peg leg and an eye patch. One glare from his single eye could turn a young recruit into a heap of feathers.

"Okay, which one of ye is ready to prove that he's worthy of the name pirate?" Patch pointed one his crooked claws at a pirate "scarecrow."

Okay mates. "Avast ye" means stop or hold fast. A baggywrinkle is an old rope used to prevent chafing or rubbing of sails.

At this moment, Gabe, Ponce, and Francisco arrive at the training site and catch the angry eye of Patch.

"How about these lazy landlubbers? Late as usual!

Landlubber is an inexperienced sailor. Dancing the "hempen jig" is the pirate term for the hangman's noose.

"I'll show everyone how it's done," bragged Francisco. Cisco was known as the island's biggest show off.

The "Captain's Challenge" was a test of a parrot's skill to take off, fly and land softly on a "captain's shoulder." Even a slight claw mark on the coat, could leave a parrot "dancing the "hempen jig."

Cisco launched himself off the pedestal and soared high in the air. Just as he was going to land, a playful seagull swooped in and scared him off.

Then it was Gabe's turn. He took off gracefully and did three acrobatic rolls before landing perfectly on the scarecrow's shoulder. His fellow cadets applauded and Gabe scored all 10's on the judges' cards.

Ponce needed a running start to get his body into the air. Like a bumblebee, he rose slowly and finally got off the ground. Much to everyone's surprise, he landed gently on the shoulder of the wooden pirate.

Then, the entire scarecrow sagged under Ponce's weight and
crumbled to the ground!
Ponce wasn't hurt. Just a few ruffled feathers.

Patch winced and scowled at Ponce with his one eye.

Meanwhile, a small parrot sits atop the high wall of the island's fort. Assigned lookout duty, he finds it hard to stay alert.

"I'm soooo bored," Little Bart said to himself. He had been on watch for 4 bells and the only things he saw on the blue horizon were some pesky seagulls and a pod of dolphins.

Looking through his trusty spyglass, his eyes suddenly grew seven and half times bigger.

On the horizon, he spotted a pirate ship "The Rusty Cutlass."

When on watch, a crew member spent four hours on duty. One stroke of the bell indicates the first half hour. Four bells means that poor Bart is only half way through his watch. Muster means to assemble especially for inspection.

Little Bart grabbed the "squawk-a-phone" – and screeched the alarm!

The townsfolk knew the meaning of the sound – cadets were to muster at the bell tower to ring the mighty bell and to flock to the dock to greet the incoming ship. The cadets quickly gathered in the bell tower. Each grabbed a part of the rope and pulled.

"Heave ho mates," shouted Ponce and the bell began to clang. Soon, all the parrots gathered at the ship's landing to give the pirates a hearty welcome to the island.

Then a mysterious figure followed Captain Sikes down the gangplank. The scary creature was Dragut, the first mate. He was a hawk with large wings and a curved beak. Patch didn't like the looks of this character.

"Fustilugs," grumbled Patch to Gabe. "Fustilugs, mean to the bone, says I."

It was Dragut, the first mate. He was a hawk with large wings and a beak that curved downward like the end of a curved dagger.

Fustilugs is an ill-natured and foul-smelling creature.

It was time for the ceremony that would decide who would become Captain Sike's parrot. The hall was packed to the rafters with all kinds of parrots – Macaws, Amazon Parrots, Pygmy Parrots, African Parrots, Black Lories, and even a few Cockatoos.

After the parrots performed the moves they learned at the academy, they stood on the long wooden perch. Sikes stood and inspected the four cadets. Francisco bowed, lifted one of his claws as a sign of respect and immediately fell to the floor. The parrots laughed when they saw that he wasn't hurt.

Ponce puffed himself up and looked too large to fit on Sike's shoulder. Little Bart also puffed himself but looked exactly the same.

The Captain pointed his finger at Gabe and bellowed, "that's the one. That's my parrot."

When Gabe's mother Martha heard that Gabe was chosen by Sikes, she was heartbroken. "He shouldn't have to be a pirate," she whimpered. She found Ponce and whispered in his ear, "Ponce you're his best friend, please keep an eye – preferably two -- on my son."

That night, Ponce hatched a plan to sneak aboard the Rusty Cutlass and check on his friend. When darkness fell, he followed a rat across the pier and quietly snuck aboard the Rusty Cutlass.

Ponce hid near the stern of the ship and listened to the snores and snorts of the sleeping pirates.

He was proud of himself for succeeding in his first mission.

That is until he shifted his weight and the bow of the ship slowly began to rise high in the sky. **"Oops,"** thought Ponce. He'd have to cut down on the crackers.

Gabe awoke and looked sleepily at the golden bars of cage. Outside, he saw a rat! A rate dressed in a pirate's clothes with a tiny sword attached to his belt.

"Hello mate, my name is Bilge."

Bilge lifted his tiny sword and with a twist of his pink hand opened the lock on the cage.

"It's okay," whispered Bilge. "I won't bite. Well, actually, I do bite, but never my friends."

"I'm Gabe"

"I know. Cap'n Sikes is just testin' you. He thinks that any parrot worthy of being his parrot should be able to escape. So that's a feather in your cap!"

Gabe looked at Bilge wondering if he could trust the rat. "Aye, but how do I know you're not a scallywag."

"Scupper that. I'd sooner be a mouse!" Gabe smiled, "All right mate, then where do I escape to?" Bilge whispered something into Gabe's ear and the parrot quickly flew out of the cage and towards an open hatch.

A scallywag is a rascal, someone who can't be trusted. "Scupper that" is something said in anger.

Dragut spread his talons and the crew became silent. He looked up at Sikes and said in a low growl. "Begging your pardon Sir, such a worthy parrot must know how to find booty. May I suggest a first mission for our newest crewmember? It will be an honor to fly with him."

Sikes pulled at his beard and said, "Aye, I think young master will find the right ship to plunder. Let it be done."

Gabe flapped his wings and soared high above the ship. Dragut was right behind him – stalking him like prey as they moved between the clouds. Gabe looked down and saw the masts of a merchant ship in the sea below.

Once again, Gabe's conscience bothered him. He didn't feel right about putting the ship in danger by alerting Dragut. Thinking fast, he distracted him with a series of quick rolls and dips.

"Soooo," cackled Dragut, "The Captain's little pet wants to play."

The faster hawk soon caught up to Gabe and gave him a menacing look. "Maybe the parrot doesn't make it back to the ship. Such a pity."

Gabe flew up and disappeared into a cloud. Then, he reappeared flying upside down facing Dragut. "Such a pity, I'll make it back to the Cutlass before you."

Gabe landed back on the ship and was surprised to find his friend Ponce surrounded by the crew. His wings were bound with rope and the chef pointed a sword at his belly.

"Blimey, this stowaway will keep us fed for a year," shouted the chef.

"Two years or more," said another.

The crew laughed until Captain Sike's ran his hook across down the mainmast. Gabe was on his shoulder whispering in his ear.

"Avast!" Sikes glared at the crew. "Stop. I'll decide when the eating is to be done. He's nothing but a pile of feathers. Let him go, or I will keelhaul the lot of you."

Keelhaul means to punish a sailor by dragging him through the water under the keel of a ship.

The next morning, a large ship with a Jolly Roger flying pulled along side the Cutlass and four pirates came aboard. It was the Neptune's Revenge. Captain Sikes bowed to the pirate with a colorful parrot on her shoulder. Gabe couldn't take his off the parrot. He knew that there was something special about this parrot.

Sikes's turned to the crew and said, "This is the captain of the Neptune – Pearl de Montauban – and mind me boys, she's as treacherous as me."

Pearl de Montauban was the daughter of a naval captain who helped lead the French to a great victory during the Battle of Beachy Head. Smart and athletic she wanted a career in the navy, but women were not allowed to join a ship's crew.

She cleverly disguised herself as a man and joined the French navy. When Pearl was finally caught, she escaped and became a pirate. It was long before she won battle after battle and earned the respect of all the pirates of the Caribbean.

He escorted Pearl to the top deck and she told him a horrible secret. "My spies have told me that many parrots have gone missing and that Dragut is behind it." Sike's replied, "I trust Dragut, he's always been loyal."

Perhaps Sikes, but keep an eye out, whispered Pearl. My parrot Fabiola swears it's the truth and I believe her.

"I will look into it. But first, perhaps my ship's fine musician's can entertain m'lady with her favorite seafaring ditties?"

While the crew was celebrating, Dragut and four mates snuck away and disappeared down the hatch.

" Tis time," snarled Dragut. "The Cutlass will soon be in our hands and Sikes and Pearl will be in in chains. We'll capture all the parrots so no other pirate will have one but us. It's not mutiny, it's our destiny."

Hidden on a beam overhead was Bilge, listening to every word.

Dragut puffed out his chest and barked an order, "take our prisoners to Isla Niebla. Soon, all of Parrot Island will be ours too."

Bilge slipped away and told Gabe and Ponce about Dragut's plot. Gabe scratched his head thinking and then hatched a plan.

"Ponce, you and Bilge need to fly home and warn my father."

Ponce nervously grabbed his crackers and began nibbling."

"My friend, I know you can do it. I believe in you Ponce!"

I will stay with Captain Sikes and see if we can escape from Isla Niebla. I know the secret caves there." Bilge handed Gabe his little dagger and whispered. "Keep safe."

Bilge scampered up Ponce's wing. Ponce flapped his wings and slowly took off and flew over the endless sea. Looking back on the Cutlass as they flew away Bilge saw Dragut's men seize Gabe, Sikes, Pearl and Fabiola.

Sikes glared at Dragut. "You broke the pirate's oath which you swore on the axe." You will be found and face our justice."

"Oh, my poor Sikes, screetched Dragut. "You will face the justice of a locked cage. I will rule the seas with all the parrots at my command."

Dragut and his pirate crew took the prisoners to the cave on their secret island. In a large cell, dozens of parrots clung to the rusted iron bars. The parrots were happy to see their old comrade Gabe. He then noticed his pal "Little Bart" was among the hostages. "What are we going to do Gabe?"

Gabe flew to the top of the cage and calmly said, "My father taught me never to give up. Never surrender. We will find a way out!" Even Sikes was impressed and smiled back at the young parrot.

Fabiola flew around looking for a way to escape.

"Gabe, if we could just pick the lock we could release everyone!" Gabe was surprised. His face turned the same red as his feathers. He didn't think Fabiola knew his name.

He glanced up at the huge door and again scratched his head. "The bars are too close together...we can't reach the lock but..."

Gabe grabbed Little Bart and gave him a big hug. "But...I think I know someone who can."

Ponce had rallied the remaining parrots back at Parrot Island and now flew out of the grey mist – with Bilge holding out his tiny dagger. Patch, Franciso, and Sir Cyril flew on either side of him. Other parrots flew behind them holding coconuts beween their claws.

High above the Rusty Cutlass the parrots led by Ponce and Bilge began dropping the coconuts on the sleepy pirates. Patch landed on the deck and used his peg leg as a sword.

Suddenly, an angry Dragut appeared on deck and confronted Gabe and Fabiola.

The parrots quickly scattered but Gabe and Fabiola stood their ground. Dragut screeched, "So if it isn't the two love birds. I should have clipped your wings when I had the chance."

"Dragut, I think you've underestimated the bravery of parrots." He whispered to Fabiola and before Dragut could react, flew quickly to the crow's nest.

An angry Dragut chased him. Just as Dragut was about to grab Gabe, a large net was suddenly dropped over the hawk by the parrots led by Fabiola and Francisco. Dragut was captured!

A crow's nest is a structure in the upper part of the mast ship used as a lookout point.

With Dragut defeated the Great Parrot Hall filled with parrots. Gabe sat in one of the regal chairs and above him perched Ponce with Bilge on his back, Francisco, and Little Bart. Sir Cyril stood on the compass and spoke.

"My fellow brothers and sisters, together we saved Parrot Island! We showed the world the true power of courage and loyalty. We have decided from this day forward, that we will not be used by the pirates to help them plunder and steal. Our cause will always be a noble one."

The parrots celebrated their newfound freedom.

Gabe and Fabiola gazed out on the endless blue ocean and dreamed about the adventures ahead.

CPSIA information can be obtained
at www.ICGtesting.com
Printed in the USA
LVHW070127210820
663782LV00034B/886